Stubborn as a Turmeric Stain

A Collection of Poems

Sheema Huq

Copyright © 2024 Sheema Huq All rights reserved.

The right of Sheema Huq to be identified as author of the book has been asserted in accordance with the Copyright and Patents Act, 1988.

ISBN: 979-8-3007-8243-6

For the fine folk
who I am very grateful
to have in my life.

CONTENTS

Acknowledgements.. i
Introduction... iii

PART I

MY BANGLADESHI ROOTS
South Asian on All Occasions... 1
The Travelling Sari.. 1

AMMA-JI
Mother's Memories... 2
Amma-Ji.. 3
Those Are Her Hands... 3

RAIN
It Can Rain with an Adrenaline.. 4
Rain-Bearing Eyes... 5
Pouring Rapture.. 5
Sorrowful Rain.. 5
A Dull Pouring of Ennui... 6
Petrichor.. 6

IMPRESSIONS OF LONDON
Something about London.. 6
Our Pledge.. 7
The Busker at Waterloo.. 8
Where There Used to Be the Weeping Willow Tree................... 8

POEM ON A PAGE
Goblet of River... 9
Lines and Dots.. 10
October Leaf... 10

CAFÉ COMEDY
Café Twaddle.. 11
In a Café by the Sea... 11

AUTUMN
Autumn Candour.. 12
A Spectacularly Brief Moment on an Autumn's Day.................. 12
Falling for Autumn... 13

BIRDS
A Skylark Sings.. 14
Birdd Textt... 15
Pink Pelicans... 15

PART II

TO SLEEP OR NOT TO SLEEP?
Busily Dreaming.. 19
Not Quite Waking Up from Her Deep Sleep....................................... 19
A Glint of Light... 19
At Approximately 2.40am.. 20
Slow Slumbering... 20

PEN AND PAPER
Paper Nature... 21
The Papery Room.. 22
This Paper... 23
This Pen.. 23

EXPERIMENTAL WORDPLAY
Beside the Cactus... 23
Too Well.. 24
At the Heart of.. 24
The Dead Fly in Her Lime Cordial and Soda Water.......................... 25
In a Bag She Never Carried.. 25
What's More to Say?... 26
The Bus Ride.. 26
This Poem Has No Title.. 27
From One Poem to Another.. 28
Would You Care for Any?... 28
I Saw You Somehow... 29

ROBOTIC RAMBLES
No, I'm Not a Robot.. 29
Yes, I'm Probably a Robot.. 30

THE SKIES ABOVE
Sky of Art.. 30
Blemished Sky.. 31
Eternal Sky.. 31

FELINE TIME
This Cat's Purrticular Intuition... 32

A Cat's Meow or Maow?... 32
Orange... 33

PART III

THE HARSHEST OF TIMES
All at Odds... 37
Tears.. 37
The Dowdiness of Days That Passed.. 37
Some Trees That I Meet.. 38
Sometime Ago or Thereabouts.. 39
After the Procedure... 39
Caved-In.. 41
Far from Near... 41
There She Sat... 42
Three Days.. 43
A Melancholic Song.. 44

WINTER
A Winter Note.. 44
Coughing Words to Myself.. 45
Oh, Bare Trees!... 45
Snowflakes.. 45
Winter Trees... 46
Late Winter Daffodils... 46
Winter Breath... 47
The Loudness of Inaudible Sound.. 47

SPRING
Beginnings and Ends.. 48
Confetti of the Cherry Blossoms... 49
Spring Bright.. 50

PART IV

THE MOON AND THE STARS
Golden Moon.. 53
In Reach... 53
Reassuring the Moon.. 53
The Stars.. 54

WITHIN MOMENTS
Those Fleeting Dandelion Days.. 55
Four Moments of My Youth... 55

This Partial Engagement.. 56
In This Moment: One to Twelve.. 57

LET THERE BE PEACE!
Peace.. 59
Bejewelled Earth... 59
Dear Ones... 60
Stillness Speaks.. 60
Tenderer Times... 60
The Dewdrops of Dawn.. 61
A Tiny New Shoot of a Blessing... 61
Great Dreams.. 61

AN ECLECTIC SELECTION
Well, Isn't This Nice?... 62
The Tiffin Carrier of Affinities... 63
My Chutney.. 64
Looking Forward.. 64
Waiting Room... 65
On the Coastal Path.. 65
Striding through the Seasons (with My Walking Group)................. 66
Alpha Awwhs.. 66
Ring of Peridot... 67
Bits of Bits.. 67
A Note to the Editors... 68
Her Fuchsias of Fuchsia... 68
Crystal.. 69
A Button for Bliss.. 69
These Doubts... 69
Hidden in Her Conscience... 70
Something Years Young!... 70
My Favourite Discontinued Scent... 71
Tea.. 72
Words... 72
Love Can Be... 73

Author's Notes... 75
About the Author... 77

Acknowledgements

Key roles in the production of this book are attributed to a few dear friends, without whom this poetry collection would not have been published. Firstly, I am incredibly grateful to my neighbour Celia Blair, a long-retired university lecturer in primary education, for sharing her invaluable editorial wisdom. Secondly, my huge appreciation goes to a regular collaborator of mine - pianist and composer Richard Calder, for his meticulous editorial advice. Thirdly, my heartfelt gratitude goes to published poet and graphic design artist Rhona Mcferran, for deftly designing and formatting this book. Lastly, a special thanks goes to poet, Manpreet Kaur for allowing for the use of an extract from her lovely review of my poem, 'Autumn Candour' in the synopsis of this book.

Introduction

I have noticed how the medium of poetry in particular, can take a plethora of diverse creative forms, subjects and styles and indeed can be written competently by anyone of any age. Poetry I believe has an egalitarian nature to it. it often suits a wide range of tastes and can have great therapeutic merit, both for the reader and the poet. This probably is what drew me to writing it in the first place.

All but one of the poems in this book have been written over the past 7 years or so. Amongst my more uplifting, experimental, observational and comical poetry I have also included a section in this book called, 'The Harshest of Times'. It has a range of poems that stylistically express the gritty elements of hardship and sadness. Such poetry is undoubtedly as reflective of the human condition as any other poems about different facets of life. All in all, I do hope sincerely that this collection offers a spectrum of poems that the reader will find stimulating and enjoyable.

Sheema Huq

October 2024

Part I

MY BANGLADESHI ROOTS

South Asian on All Occasions

I'm South Asian
on all occasions!

All day, every day
and on vacations!

A sitarist strums to
tablas in my brain!

I'm as stubborn as
a turmeric stain!

I get so drenched
in masala chai rain!

Red chilies run all
through my veins!

The Travelling Sari

Her whims keep
swerving
        and straying
and sauntering
and pottering,
 with
        gatherings
 and imaginings
    neatly pleated
and tucked in

Those capers and
occurrences
    keep perilously
unravelling,
as quests shall
digress, before
drifting and
    ever rambling.

Many trials are
constantly
dawdling and
    ambling, and
dreams that
are draped keep
    jolting and
stammering.

    As deeds can't
help but
gape prior to
    meandering, and
what's plain
    seems unfazed,
when
swaying
    while travelling.

AMMA-JI

Mother's Memories

My mother would brush her teeth and make them sparkle with a toothbrush made from a twig of a Neem Tree and a piece of charcoal. She washed pots

and pans in their droves with the ashes
from the wood fire of the earthen stove.
Mother learned her first English words,
 "Morning School", which she attended
aged seven as a weary pupil. In a big
circle under a Mango Tree, the children
sat curiously. Teacher was very strict,
and no child wore shoes. Learning was
fun, shaded from a red sun, and they
weren't aware that resources were few!

Amma-Ji

(A Bengali term, marking a show of respect for one's mother)

Amma   Amma   Amma   Amma-Ji!
I don't love you any less than you love me.
Amma   Amma   Amma   Amma-Ji!
I'll bring a measuring jug so you shall see,
Amma   Amma   Amma   Amma-Ji!
that the fondest love, flows immeasurably!
Amma   Amma   Amma   Amma-Ji
The only thing to do is to pour more tea!

Those Are Her Hands

Those are her hands
that have tended to a lifetime of plants
that have prized pomegranates apart
that willingly provide and gratefully receive
that wave about demonstratively

Those are her hands
that don't use an iPad or self-service machine
that fill her mouth with betel nuts and leaves

that have held her holy books to devour and read
that have replied to letters from across
the oceans and seas

Those are her hands
that determinedly organised and agreed
that have been dismayed and have offered relief
that would wash her clothes in a nearby stream
that would pick ripe physalis from the village trees

Those are her hands
that have cooked delicious curries
that have worked arduously in factories
that have massaged aching feet
that have fanned herself in stifling heat

Those are her hands
that have endlessly tidied after and cleaned
that have sewn numerous seams
that have prayed with unfaltering belief
that have nurtured and grieved

RAIN

It Can Rain with an Adrenaline

It can rain with an adrenaline,
that brings a comforting sense of
'a lack of the lack of everything',
and a blurry hope that this gushing
spell of divine prosperity will
wash away the relentlessness of
countless, baleful uncertainties.

Rain-Bearing Eyes

All across her mind was a
foreboding sky where the
sun never shone and birds
did not fly. Rain-bearing
clouds would drift through
her reticent eyes, pouring
grief over a bleak horizon
of hollow cheeks, on to
dispirited lips that could
not speak. It was after a
few months that a gentler
phase had at last come.
As she sought relief in her
overarching belief in a
radiant, recrudescent sun.

Pouring Rapture

Pouring rapture reconvenes,
as a crescendo of rainfall
washes a melodic sanctity
upon a bustling rural scene.
Gushing on to livelihoods,
a fresh symphony of being.

Sorrowful Rain

the rain pours out its heart with
skilful art
into the lake and river that ache
far apart.
the rain falls with voluminous
might from

a sky of pewter and white. how
without any
sight of blue, this sky cries for   you.

A Dull Pouring of Ennui

This dismal, blurry, lethargic,
sulking, drenched monotony
may not intend to last for all
eternity. However, just in case
it does, let's meet thereafter.

Petrichor

Could it be that we'll really,
very nearly, almost, never
have the foremost chance
of very almost never, really
ever, nearly reuniting soon,   at last?

IMPRESSIONS OF LONDON

Something about London

London is bursting with
stories and is piled high
with worries in the varied
vicinities of local and
global societies where
we are all as bland and
as ordinary as we are
tragic or ecstatic, and

perhaps neither of those or
too otherwise engaged.

And too out of pocket or
too tired to be preoccupied
by the grandeur and
the most extraordinary.
During rush hour when
life is intense and the
populace is as dense as it
is excessively impersonal,
we do what we might
as well, which is to pretend
that it is - not at all.

In this vast City where
we can be tiny and small
amidst the vistas that
are as great and as grand
and as tall as the shrinking
glories and crammed-in
woes, and whilst there
are parts of London where
the vibrancy is immense,
we may not know who
lives just over the fence.

Our Pledge

D-a-i-l-y c-o-m-m-u-t-i-n-g -i-n- t-h-e c-i-t-y
o-f L-o- n-d-o-n w-i-l-l p-r-o-v-i-d-e e-v-e-r-y
c-o-n-c-e-i-v-a-b-l-e t-y-p-e- -o-f- p-e-r-s-o-n
w-i-t-h a-m-p-l-e o-p-p-o-r-t-u-n-i-t-i-e-s t-o
k-n-o-w **a totally congested** i-s-o-l-a-t-i-o-n.

The Busker at Waterloo

There's a low pitched, hurried, gasping sequence of broken phrases. While the singer beguiles many with impromptu gazes. She abruptly changes tempo as she sways in confluence with the wind. My heart beats even faster as the cold air tingles against my skin. Losing all sense of time fondly seems akin to the mesmeric rawness of her adrenaline.

Where There Used to Be the Weeping Willow Tree

There used to be the weeping willow tree as we entered King George's Park, near the stone bridge and the lake. Now it's no longer there to swing and shake. The perky, peckish pigeons still come in their hoards.

The ducks and moor hens, still barely seem bored. Courtly swans float by, as bright as the sky, as a coot calls out toward a mallard's brash and incredulous cry, by the spot where there used to be the weeping willow tree.

POEM ON A PAGE

Goblet of River

Processions of volitional waves emerge, roaring, teasing, lavish, as rapidly as they are to entirely diminish. With the broken ray of sun at high noon follow subtle streams of differing fortunes. Drifting in to a conscious realm of shadowy rippled reflections,
stillness,
soulful
lulling
alone
y e t
n o t
a t
a l l
! ! !

Lines and Dots

Line and dot and line and Dot
put their little baby in a cot

!._!

and as their little baby grew
his cot broke into two

!.__ ./

and when they tried to mend
the cot they couldn't align
the Line with the Dot

!.__ .l

October Leaf

        A
     disused,
          diverging
  belief
             falls
with
          subtle
  grief.
         Settling
     with the
        softness
         of
           delicate
              relief.

CAFÉ COMEDY

Café Twaddle

My fingertips are acrobats that
click and tap and press and hit
on claptrap that's nondescript.
I scroll down and take a look at
piffle, guff and gobbledygook.
I buy a tea and pay in cash and
return to reading balderdash.
My friend arrives at 9.30 (-ish)
and I greet them with some
gibberish. And we dribble on
like paragons of hooey, phooey
tommyrot, as we finish off with
a lot of flapdoodle poppycock!

In a Café by the Sea

By the port with two ships,
two lips took
two sips of rosehip tea, at
a table with
tulips in a cafe by the sea.
Every table had
two lips, taking two sips of
rosehip tea,
sipping glumly by the tulips
in the quiet bit
of a dim lit cafe by the sea.

AUTUMN

Autumn Candour

Rustic hues
grace the
views with
copious
surrender;

feet trudge
instinctively
through
captivating
texture.

Vivid shades
are on
parade, in
bountiful
dimensions,

with gusty,
sunlit
accolades to
tumbling
expressions.

A Spectacularly Brief Moment on an Autumn's Day

Valiantly swirling rust leaves
rose from the
              ground eagerly
floating and fleeting, swaying
upwards and outwards with
a vexatious breeze!

                    Conveying
the divinest artistry of being
somewhat, rather furiously
                    aggrieved!
Then settling
         terribly hurriedly, as if
stillness was urgently in need.
Spectacularly brief
         were these actions of
quiet compliance,
              ornamental defiance,
and spur of the moment grief.

Falling for Autumn

The
                    rust
covered
         leaves
                    were
 to know
      it was
                    not
their
                    pride
that
      had
              fallen,
     despite
descending
          in rueful
motions,
with
                    each
inevitable
          expulsion.
Then
    settling

    in a
                manner
    that
              was
    whimsically
          gamesome,
    with
              but
    a vague,
        jaunty
            notion
    of the
        capricious
    temperament
    of mid-
           Autumn.

BIRDS

A Skylark Sings

I heard what sounded like a meandrous instrument, one warm emerging Spring, from a crested bird with streaked wings. As I listened to the Skylark alluringly sing, the melodic notes of this brown and taupe creature were to mesmerically ring. What a fine, meditative presence upon the land it did bring. Time that was considerably enthralling - graced by its bountiful calling. Alas, it is today a much rarer thing.

Birdd Textt

Yuu wwitth yourrr
dafftt fingerrtipps
unttethered, dddo
pleassze excusse
my texct errorss!
Yu shudd asume,
neverreverr thattt
Ii'm nottt exacttly
cleverr,, aass yuu
allso tryy typingg
wiith yourr bbeak
ffor onnee weekk
whenn sccurying
arround, makiing
awkardd soundss
az a faastt, ffussy
peccker of eachh
lettr, whliist clapiin
flaapingg tthhose
thingz calld wingz
andd rufffliing yrr
fflouncy featthrrs!

Pink Pelicans

There's no telling them,
those pink pelicans,
that they're pelicans
who are dazzling while
they're wandering
and gandering!

There's no telling them,
those pink pelicans,
that they're pelicans

who love chilling while
they're dawdling
then lingering!

There's no telling them,
those pink pelicans,
that they're pelicans
who are thrilling while
they're mooching
and fidgeting!

As we'll be telling them,
those pink pelicans,
when they're far too
busy loafing, whilst
knowing almost
everything!

Part II

TO SLEEP OR NOT TO SLEEP?

Busily Dreaming

Might she unsee what
she is seeing and unbe
what she is being, while
time itself is leaving
through the tiny cracks
in the ceiling? A distant
voice is calling as she
grapples with what she
is gleaning from the
different fragments of
all the aspects of those
convoluted meanings.

Not Quite Waking Up from Her Deep Sleep

With a fumbling stumble she attempts
to untangle her jittering jumble of rambling
grumbles that waffle and babble with
murmurs and mumbles from the mangling
shambles of muffling prattle as she
utters her muddles with bumbling shuffles.

A Glint of Light

I know I have had a good sleep
during the dearth of glowing
mirth in the darkness of pre-
dawn. As I wake to realise my
rest's colossal worth with dozy

yawns. Only to find its full value
depletes, while a glint of light
defeats its rejuvenating magic,
when my alarm remorselessly
and coarsely calls at early morn.

At Approximately 2.40am

My poem doesn't care to be
a poem which gets admired
when read, so it's a rhyme
that's too perfectly, absurdly
fatuous instead; and might
possibly be a kind of rhyme
you won't ever recall, for it's
not a "proper" rhyme at all!

It shan't mention a great sea
or terrain or my inescapable
pressures or unwitting gains.
Rather, it's a sleep deprived
attempt to keep my wakeful
self entertained, as I dwell on
unfounded details to amend

(and so here is its sleeplessly
bed-bound, indefinite end!).

Slow Slumbering

Slow slumbers of
hankering and
slipping into the
sunken sinking
of a heavy inkling

that deepens
when deepening
by seemingly
unseeing the
seeping streaming
of subconsciously
being with the
fragility of the
feelings filtering
deeper and
deepening in through
to the perplexing
unknowing of
what is for keeping
and what is for
deleting, prior to the
event of waking.

PEN AND PAPER

Paper Nature

As I plucked the pods of
Peas from the purple
paper Trees, a peculiarly
pinkish patterned Leaf fell
to my floaty, flimsy feet,
so thin and papery. And
it was with the chaotic
monologue of the paper
tissue Fog that the hardy,
hidden yellow cardboard
Sun, with an agile skip
and a jovial hum, radiantly
announced, "a crisply

creased, white, crepe
paper Cloud and I who
rarely make a sound, will
do our very best to stick
around!" Then once the
Fog was removed, more
recycling had accrued,
suitable to represent the
mild, misty greyish blue
as a hefty, humid Cloud's
bleary mood and freshly
mounted Morning Dew.

The Papery Room

She keeps selectively
collecting each idealistic
belief, piece by particle,
by fragment, by portion.
Capturing chapters
and quotations, penned
over the ages, that are
found upon flimsy, floaty,
loose note pages, within
decrepit old walls of
mostly forgotten toils.

A4, mountainous, messy
hordes, of many a trial
and phase, gradually fade,
with new commotions,
into faint, ineligible greys.
These slightly crumpled
writings, of immeasurably
slipshod, ever precious,
jewel-like notions, are her
inestimable "treasuries
of introspective devotion".

This Paper

Is this one A5, plain paper piece
not as valuable as a gold leaf and
as precious as an entire mineral
mine and its grand encasing reef?

This Pen

For this pen shall quiver
while the ink does weep
and the mind will dither
yet the words still seep
when the motions slither
while the pauses sleep
by the verve that withers
as only silence speaks.

EXPERIMENTAL WORDPLAY

Beside the Cactus

Languid
clouds pose
pale and
listless,
near to
spacious,
rainless
Texas.
Pensively
restless,
with jittery

plexus,
hopeless,
hapless,
neat and
spotless.
She with
her cactus,
thorny,
fractious,
sitting
oddly on
her gluteus
maximus.

Too Well

Having known the 'aridness of barrenness'
that had an 'excessiveness of narrowness'
within the 'vast abundance of hollowness'
way deep inside a 'bottomless vacantness'
of the 'endless, vagueness of aimlessness'
buried in the 'void of absolute elusiveness',
namely, the 'laborious incompleteness of
a singularly incalculable, discomforting,
comfort, of this pure totality of blankness',

he concluded that he knew it all too well.

At the Heart of…

Whereof, All of, Thereof, To Talk of,
Glints of, The Glory of, A Portion of,
The Sake of, or Sort of, What of, That
of, Those of, In Want of, None of, or
Some of, One of, The Most of, Are of,

A Mark of, To Make of, A Kind of, As
of, The Sum of, Was of, Is of, Then of,
A Land of, Hands of, And of, an End
of, A Start of, A Part of, The Heart of.

The Dead Fly in Her Lime Cordial and Soda Water

Far from inapparent was her
subsequent abhorrence
towards a sudden morbid
presence amongst the sweet
and tangy pleasance, of such
a fluorescent, luminescent,
incessant effervescence, that
was an unattained indulgence,
during her mid-adolescence.

When, despite a shy hesitance,
she asked for a replacement,
that came to be a triumph due
to the absence of confidence,
that appeared no different from
ceasing to be existent, amid
a fluorescent, luminescent,
most effervescent pleasance,
during her mid adolescence.

In a Bag She Never Carried

In a bag she never carried to the places
where she'd never been, without all the
friends she never had, with whom she'd
never laugh, quarrel or sing, she'd kept
no notes of her non-existence, in a bag
containing her various, non-existent

things, including a smart phone she
never used, with which her unceasing
non-existence was never going to begin!

What's More to Say?

If these words appear

  to be unequivocally non-compulsory,
and superfluously
                         unnecessary,
whilst evidently,
markedly and
                         undesirably
unduly unwarranted, unessential,
expendable
surpluses, that are
        most imprudently immaterial;
whilst also, seemingly, needlessly
                       immoderately
and relentlessly, disproportionately
extra,
exorbitantly,
        non-pertinently inessential;
in addition to being irrelevantly
extraneous and invariably,
                    perpetually, tiresomely
desultory and aimlessly uneventful;

What's more to say?

The Bus Ride

She sweats in the
heat, saying, "Em, eh, em".

She's grinding her
teeth, saying, "Em, eh, em".

She finds empty
seats, saying, "Em, eh, em".

She gives her niece
a treat, saying, "Em, eh, em".

She makes herself
neat, saying, "Em, eh, em".

She's nearly at her
street, saying, "Em, eh, em".

Soon she's on her
feet, saying, "Em, eh, em".

Life is incomplete
without those "Em, eh, ems".

This Poem Has No Title

I'm afraid I have to apologize a
little, because this poem has
no title, as I actually think that
it's undeniably indefinable, that
what's intangibly unreliable is
intrinsically a mystery that's
shrouded inextricably with an
utter incomprehensibility, that's
unimpressively, unaccountably,
so annoyingly unsatisfactory,
and absolutely, resolutely what's
bewilderingly, overpoweringly
discombobulating and baffling   to me!

From One Poem to Another

Dare not stop
before my
metaphors to
spend time
with my rhymes
because
the friction on
your diction
is not a good
sign. Never
pander to my
stanzas or
stand alone
with my tone
or I'll teeter
with your metre
and have a
righteous moan.

Would You Care for Any?

What there is, is no great
sparsity of majorly barely,
and enormously scarcely,
broadly narrowly, largely
slightly, faintly massively,
vaguely mightily, hugely
paltry, colossally meagrely,
marginally vastly, mostly
hardly, soaringly sparingly,
grandly minimally, mildly
potently, eminently measly,
and ambitiously gingerly,
yet gigantically partially,
humongously weeny and

amply scanty proportions
of plenty of the minutest,
fewest of many, that are
exceedingly excessively,
necessarily unnecessary.   Would you care for any?

I Saw You Somehow

I saw you somehow in both the then and the
now. We met somewhere in the vast unaware
nowhere of unknown everywheres. A place,
neither round, rectangular, oblong nor square.
We were caught in the vicinity of the infinity of
forgotten despairs, and lost in the tomorrows
of yesterday's sorrows. Not knowing why it is
never easy to leave a world that only partially
cares, or how we arrived in this unspecified   *elsewhere.*

ROBOTIC RAMBLES

No, I'm Not a Robot

No, I'm not a robot, even though
I too can break a bar of chocolate
into perfectly precise pieces and
whatnot. Maybe peckish robots
are programmed to be resistant
to scoffing huge custard donuts,
and donning mismatching socks
is not a style they readily adopt!

Robots too must get searingly hot,
yet aren't especially, hopelessly
bad at colouring by numbers and

drawing dot to dot. Whereas, I, in
being prone to texting infrequent
afterthoughts, and with a stomach
that can be likened, to a jumbo
sugar pot……no I'm not a robot.

Yes, I'm Probably a Robot

Could this deficiency of high
efficiency sufficiently suffice?
As I assiduously, and most
meticulously, try to be precise?
Though, might I attempt to be,
unreservedly, symmetrically
aligned with my desire to be,
so emphatically, absolutely spot
on time? Particularly, when I'd
rather be intrinsically leading
a flawlessly exacting life, that's
entirely free of unpredictability
and a feeble attempt to rhyme!

THE SKIES ABOVE

Sky of Art

I trudged through the park before
it got dark, as the late afternoon
was to soon depart. The sky was
a canvas of rich smouldering grey,
blazing, rouge sparks with golden
parts, glowing like shards of glass.
The combined drama was raging,
engaging, and beguiling yet stark.

I trudged through the park before
it got dark, with my eyes upon the
artful sky, and my head in my heart.

Blemished Sky

A bruised sky spews
unwelcome truths upon us.
Swamping certitude.

Eternal Sky

Eternal sky of cloudy white,
behind the woollen mounds of
fluff are spectrums of mystery,
of wonder, of glorious light.

Eternal sky of gold and red,
spirited extravagance seeps
through fleeting shimmers,
embellishing every thread.

Eternal sky of seamless blue,
without a single cloud in view,
whispering that peace and
harmony can become true.

Eternal sky of murky grey,
postponing such fantabulous
promises, until a hopeful and
cherished moment of the day.

FELINE TIME

This Cat's Purrticular Intuition

If I'll never be what I rarely
am and I barely am what I
seldom can, as I merely can
when I always know that I
ought to know when I shall
climb and go, or ignore it
all, to curl up in a cosy ball,
without fail - nose to tail,
unaware of stormy gales!

A Cat's Meow or Maow?

I tend to sense, somehow, that
a Cat's Maow is a Maow,
and is not a Meow,
when they say Hi, or guess
Why or even How!

Don't you reckon, somehow, that
a Cat's Maow is a Maow,
and is not a Meow, as they
express a weary Aye, Eh,
or uninspired Oh?

Surely we all see, somehow, that
a Cat's Maow is a Maow,
and is not a Meow, as
they make a high pitched
Plea or 'take a Bow'?

I'm prone to think somehow, that
a Cat's Maow is a Maow,

and is not a Meow, as they
declare, "Ciao, I'm wholly
unavailable right now!"

Orange

He was the burliest Cat I ever did know
and curliest Cat I ever did see!

The surliest Cat ever on show, who was
shrouded with a quaint mystery!

He had the furriest back ever to grow,
did the purriest Cat in history!

Part III

THE HARSHEST OF TIMES

All at Odds

Weeds of mistrust
grew from the ground
while isolation was to
always be around.

Droplets of anguish
fell from the sky while
peace and justice
were a perpetual lie.

The still, peevish air
was thick with fear
while nothing at all
could be held dear.

Tears

Just as there are quite a few more
stars in the universe than there are
grains of sand; far greater tears of
hurt and sorrow are shed, than can
be tenderly wiped away by hands.

The Dowdiness of Days That Passed

Drab were her statements upon
   the dullness of the pavements,
beneath the dense
        dreariness of the skies

seen by disillusioned and dire
eyes; during
    the banality of glum greys of
  never-ending, harsh, overcast
          days after days
after days. Consecutive days
 of bleak, week upon week upon
week upon week.
    The despairing dowdiness of
the days that passed
wasn't to last and last, wasn't to   last.

Some Trees That I Meet

There are tatty
trees which are
batty trees, that
are crass, bare
and ratty trees.

They gloat at
you. They glare
at me. As rain
weeps upon the
wintry streets.

These tatty trees,
which are batty
trees, that are
crass and bare
and ratty trees.

They gloat at
you. They glare
at me and pose
with grotesque
authenticity.

Those tatty trees,
which are batty
trees, that are
crass and bare
and ratty trees.

They gloat at
you. They glare
at me. They
can't help their
scowling misery.

Sometime Ago or Thereabouts

I blended into the drab
grey of the paved ground,

as I moped with the
aloofness of sombre clouds.

While I shed tears that
merged with drizzling rain,

as the wind did swiftly
meld into the hollow pain.

After the Procedure

With the hush
of turbulence
shifting in me

I was lost
in the lull of

a cloudless
obscurity

Unduly
immersed in
my soundless
fragility

A senseless
silence kept
running to me

As a heavy
stillness
was sinking
through me

The daunted
quietness
calmed
me nearly

A pensive
calmness
jostled by me

A cold
numbness
was prancing
fiercely

A pained
compliance
would nest
within me

With the hush
of turbulence
all around me

I was lost
in the lull of
a cloudless
obscurity

Caved-In

He's on the inside of the outside
of the outskirts from within the
stone walls from long ago, before
he began to begin, to be carved
out of silent shouts by becoming
too caved-in, while no amount of
working out would console the

whole
of
him.

Far from Near

She slowly whispers
in the ears of
buried fears that try
hard not to
be here, when there
is a minor
chance of a glance
that seems to
know what it wants,
and what
it wants is for all of
her tears to
disappear into those

inordinate,
non-existent years
of a mightily
ample time of cheer,
that belong
nowhere, other than
somewhere
that is far from near,
and only too
indecisively unclear
of a hope that
quite idly reappears.

There She Sat

Her skin crept
in.

Her
  bones
     collapsed   out.

There
she sat, an

   empty mass

of
her own self-
      doubt.

Nothing was
    ever said

while
  every organ

played

dead,

    repeatedly,
defeatedly,

       in her
sullen

          head.

Three Days

If today
were
yesterday
and two
days
after
yesterday
were
not
tomorrow,
what
happened
to
whom,
when
and how -
she
could not
claim
to follow.
This
absence

of a
sense
of
knowing -
she
hoped
would
numb
her sorrow.

A Melancholic Song

It doesn't feel entirely wrong to climb
deep inside a melancholic song and
reside there, with old memories that
are worn and threadbare, as a mood
of sorrow gathers dust and the mind
aims to regain its peace and trust.
The misty moon's mystique lingers on
while waves of the sea surge beyond
the dejected tone of a sombre song.

WINTER

A Winter Note

It was after we had increased our
pace and exhaled that we noted
how exulting variations of winter's
voiceless articulations prevailed!

Coughing Words to Myself

Cough up your phlegm of ambivalence!
Sneeze your bacteria of unease!
Blow an indignant prose from your nose!
But do use a fresh tissue please!

Oh, Bare Trees!

Bare are their branches, and brash is their bark! Firm and pronounced, elegant and stark. These entwined and entangled exhibits of scant parks serve to define winter's chilly start. So dreamily ornamental are their silhouettes in the dark. As their wistful, wintertide tales reach out to open hearts. Oh, Bare Trees, you're living works of art!

Snowflakes

These chaotic commuters
of the freezing cold air fall
sporadically to destination
anywhere. Some clash
until they dizzily dash and
settle in silence. The rest
make a fuss while drifting
with determined avoidance.
Flurries of copious energy
drop disconcertedly with an
impassioned conscience
desperate for the ground!

Winter Trees

It is when the Winter's golden Sun
is graciously glowing
While the shifting, silvery Skies are
sumptuously snowing
And the whimsical, warrior Winds
are brazenly blowing
As the roving, redemptive Waters
are fervently flowing
That, with a contemplative knowing,
bare, satisfied Trees
praise the scenes that are showing.

Late Winter Daffodils

Through late Winter's bitterest chill, Spring instils its striking will; blazing golden, starry thrills of trumpets blowing their dainty frills. Some of the starkest sights were devoid of delight, until the emergence of delicate daffodils. Quaintly pleasant, with a distinct presence; so graciously simple.

Soon they shall tilt, then wilt and wither away. Facing what is one day inevitable. Rendering their perfect, present bloom, through the freezing gloom, momentarily invaluable. As for now, these sunny heads of yellow lustre do gently rock with rhythmic flusters to the ever changing, flurrying blusters.

Winter Breath

      Cold climate
            occurrences
     which
         appear
      to be
   monumentally
     rare
       are
     those
   vanishing,
            chilly plumes
    of our
       breath,
    that
        emerge in
     the
    biting
       air.
             Exposing
      the
    lyrical
   evanescence
   of being
        entirely
       present,
  nowhere
    else
       but
    there.

The Loudness of Inaudible Sound

Bitter
cold air, an unadorned ground.
Bare

branches yawn at pale, silvery clouds.
The barren silence is pristinely loud.

SPRING

Beginnings and Ends

Spring's beginnings
Winter's ends

Beginnings of beginnings
Beginnings of ends
Ends of debris
Beginnings of new leaves

Spring's beginnings
Winter's ends

Raw green beginnings
Demised remains descend
Beginnings of new things
merging with ends

Spring's beginnings
Winter's ends

Endings and beginnings
Interim friends
Sprouting and emerging
with endings of ends

Spring's beginnings
Winter's ends

Spring's beginnings
Winter's ends

Confetti of the Cherry Blossoms

floaty, tendersome
see them, know them
shed some, show some
fleeting, short term
the wind will blow them

Confetti of the Cherry Blossoms

hesitant, hurrisome
drifting motions
lay some, hold some
catch them, throw them
sprinkle or spatter some

Confetti of the Cherry Blossoms

quivering, wondersome
see them, know them
shed some, show some
lay some, hold some
the sun glows on them

Confetti of the Cherry Blossoms

wispy, scattersome
find some, hide some
catch some, throw some
gone for certain
strewn and fallen

Confetti of the Cherry Blossoms

huddling, lingersome
take one, feel one
shed some, show some
fleeting, short term
the rain will soak them

Confetti of the Cherry Blossoms

Spring Bright

As the sun glistened
on the rippled lake,
the mallards entered
into fractious debates,
argy-bargy, kerfuffle,
then silence
after a halt.
Yet the little observers
couldn't decide who
was at fault.
Not quite holus-bolus
was the quiet,
on a chilly spring day,
so utterly bright.
Even brighter than the
busyness of busy
grown-up lives,
than of impassioned
mallards' strife.

Part IV

THE MOON AND THE STARS

Golden Moon

Last night the full Moon looked
resplendently golden, from a
road with a name in a location
that I've thoroughly forgotten.
I should go there more often.

In Reach

The stars and the moon
in their glory gleam with
radiance in the distance,
amidst the smoky grey
clouds that seem to barely
drift while their glowing
persists, until they vanish
from my conscious view,
and maybe won't be lost
again soon, now that they're
in reach, upon a pink tatty
note sheet in a lofty room.

Reassuring the Moon

The whole Moon was in
a hazy, blushing conflict
with the clouds. Convinced
it was only scarcely able
to endow its shimmering,
glassy vows. As it pulled the

tide with frustrated sighs,
the Sea replied, "Oh, why
should you care to sigh? For
whichever phase you're in,
be it full, three quarters, or
half, a third, a quarter, or
a distinctive crescent...
whether or not you have
a largely obscured, pale,
misty or a stupendously
bright, glowing presence;
I flow, and I reverberate
to your mystical, alluring
light. It is you, dear Moon,
who bestows the night!"

The Stars

Glowing
distant
balls of
hydrogen
and
helium
sparkle
with
divinely
superb
elated
delirium!

WITHIN MOMENTS

Those Fleeting Dandelion Days

Faint, fluffy fragments of
a childhood's frivolity float
far.... into this moment.

Four Moments of My Youth

The moment I thought
that my friends wouldn't
care soon vanished like
a whisper in the air.

And the rhythms of
change were to unfurl
in this teetering,
slippery, rickety world.

The moment I realised
that they'd understand
was like a downpour
of rain on arid land.

And the rhythms of
change were to unfurl
in this teetering,
slippery, rickety world.

The moment I knew
that they'd all gone
was as if the daylight
became withdrawn.

And the rhythms of
change were to unfurl

in this teetering,
slippery, rickety world.

The moment I was to
see them again, our
sunny hopes glistened
on the River Thames.

And the rhythms of
change were to unfurl
in this teetering,
slippery, rickety world.

This Partial Engagement

So brief is my state that cares to engage with
        a quaint moment of
                grace. As devouring sun
rays disperse a warm and persistent embrace.

The silent wind gently lingers
                upon my face as I inhale the
scents of spring on the open
                space. An impromptu rhythm
    evolves within my own
pace. Sometimes our entitlements occur
            without a trace. For this seems
to be the
condition of everyday fate: for us to have and
then to
     disown a sensation of many sensations
 in a particular
                time and place,
or for some to be
captured in speech or writing or hidden within
a Facebook page.

I, myself

remain
partially engaged
      with this
moment
of Grace.

In This Moment: One to Twelve

In This Moment – I

The leaves outside keep
shimmying with salsa vibes.

In This Moment – II

A cluster of damp trees on the high street
exudes the aroma of a lush, coniferous forest.

In This Moment – III

As I board a bus, so rouge and rectangular,
finding a seat couldn't be more unspectacular.

In This Moment – IV

A grey cat projects the fathomless
stillness of a permanent fixture.

In This Moment – V

I am fulfilled by innately benign banalities.

In This Moment – VI

I put a shell against my ear and listen
to the echoes of a befouled sea.

In This Moment – VII

Everything is present apart from unpolluted air.

In This Moment – VIII

A procession of waves caped in silver
ceremoniously ripples across the river.

In This Moment – IX

The rapture of June is immortalized
by the honeysuckle's scent and sight.

In This Moment – X

I breathe in the lucid calm of early dawn.

In This Moment – XI

I am entitled to be idle and entirely unvital.

In This Moment - XII

A hope has fallen and settled like a lily petal.

LET THERE BE PEACE!

Peace

It was
with the divine
artistry of azure
skies;

and the rousing
wind's
immortal cries,

and the crashing
waves
of brazen seas,

that
the will of peace
took flight to be
Free.

Bejewelled Earth

Lost legends
gleam amidst
the clouds

Forgotten lores
shimmer deep
in the sea

Bygone ballads
sparkle from
the ground

Olden couplets
glimmer upon
the trees

Dear Ones

When the tides of misfortune come,
the waves of wisdom know
that the sea and sky are one, while
the winds and waters flow.
With the stillness of the moon and
the drifting rays of sun, may
healing destinies glow for dear ones.

Stillness Speaks

Stillness speaks to weeping eyes
weeping eyes with lengthy sighs.
Dreams reside where silence lies.
Silence lies where weeping eyes
cease to weep as peace is nigh,
and quiet breaths drift softly by.

Tenderer Times

A lonely voice was humming
to an aching conscience that
was strumming. That aching
conscience kept strumming
to a broken heart that was
drumming. Until that broken
heart was drumming to the
tenderer times to be coming.

The Dewdrops of Dawn

If only the dewdrops of dawn
were our Earth's tears of relief,
for every breeze which gently
blew the essence of peace,
and as hope and solace flowed
across the oceans and seas,
each child were to know they
could fulfil precious dreams.

A Tiny New Shoot of a Blessing

When something grows where
nothing grew, and something
from nothing bestows a new
truth of seeming no less than
being no more, and becoming
as blessed as never before.
New phases shall come and
old phases shall pass while
a new shoot emerges at last.

Great Dreams

the
deserts
need the sand

like
the seas
need the land

like
the waves
need the seas

like
the birds
need the trees

like
the plants
need the bees

like
we need
great dreams!

AN ECLECTIC SELECTION

Well, Isn't This Nice?

Well, isn't this nice? So divinely nice!
Much nicer than I can say for the state of my life!
And isn't this great? So superbly great!
That agony should arrive not a minute too late!
Isn't this lovely? So especially lovely!
That I'm forgetting how to spell the word "hhapi".

How wonderfully marvellous that
all should seem disastrous!

How brilliantly stupendous that
all should seem monstrous!

Isn't this fantastic? So truly fantastic!
That I would smile readily if my lips were elastic!
Isn't this grand? So spectacularly grand!
That comedy with irony is what I cannot stand!
Isn't this fabulous? So utterly fabulous!
That times are becoming unbearably ludicrous!

How joyfully glorious that all
should seem atrocious!

How terrifically tremendous that
all should seem odious!

Isn't this beautiful? So supremely beautiful!
That my mood is getting increasingly miserable!
Isn't this splendid? So perfectly splendid!
That a problem begins as soon as one's ended!
Now isn't this fine? So delightfully fine!
That these ghastly indignities are totally mine!

The Tiffin Carrier of Affinities

A carrier of home cooked love
of sunny skies above

of antidotes to murky greys
of random thoughts of bygone days
of thinking in italics and doing in bold
of being as young as one is old
of tea gardens and fields of green
of near and far adventuring
of a red sun and translucent moon
of a high tide at high noon
of capturing a moment before it has gone
of overcoming and of moving on
of cityscapes and rural paths
of mountain tops and fresh cut grass

A carrier of home cooked dreams
of ripples of a flowing steam

of coming in from the cold
of the wonderment as a night unfolds

of the elements and constellations
of marking endless occasions
of the heartiness of one's spirit and soul
of silver linings and crops of gold
of azure waves upon grand seas
of the rays of warmth and gentlest breeze
of healing hearts as time shall pass
of making and remaking new starts
of when the sun and the moon are aligned
of tasting the blessings of a lifetime....

My Chutney

If the World and I were
boundlessly chummy,
would I make chutney
this rousing and ballsy?

And if every moment
were trivial and funny,
would I make chutney
this stirring and plucky?

If the sky were heartily,
vividly, endlessly sunny,
would I make chutney
this grasping and gutsy?

Looking Forward

He was looking
forward to much
more agreeable
times that were
wholesome and

kind and had
wilful regard for
the elusive parts...

(...that don't
necessarily rhyme!).

Waiting Room

Sitting in close
    proximity, with
        much distance
            and disharmony.
                One sucks their
                    silver spoon, as
                        the other revels in
                            misanthropic gloom.

On the Coastal Path

Waves rock.
Mud drifts.
Eroding cliff.

Paths curve.
Sparrows' nest.
Out of breath.

Brambles cut.
Stifling day.
No right of way.

Terns cry.
Diverted route.
Sandy boots.

Winds waft.
Cuttlefish bone.
Far from home.

Striding through the Seasons (with My Walking Group)

Spring's eagerness
swiftly budded, as its
chilly mopery lifted!

Summer prospects gaily
ripened, as beaming
gladness was emitted!

Autumn's pageantry
amply shedded, as its
sundry worries wilted!

Winter's toils were
covered, as our jaunty
relish stayed quilted!

Alpha Awwhs

breathe, cry, suck, sleep, wee, shriek.
tiny little hands, tiny little feet,
glance, poo, 'gaga goo',
maybe that's a smile,
nappies in a pile,
sneeze, wheeze,
laugh, sit, crawl, grip,
outdoor trip, point, wobble,
sit, fall, fleetingly monumental,
gently grappling, initiating with all.

Ring of Peridot

She wore a ring of olivine
mineral set in silver, on her
little right finger. It either came
from somewhere way up high:
in fact from out of space, a
meteorite; or it came from
somewhere relatively low:
the Earth's crust.

The lava from a volcano.
Either way, she could for
certain trust that extraordinary
peridot was her birthstone for
the August month. It could
sometimes reflect her moods.
It clashed with all her clothes,

It blended in with her skin,
matching the stud in her nose.
She knew that the eleven other
birthstones were equally as
fascinating to discover. As it goes,
she thought there could be
another kind of poem for her
kind friend to compose!

Bits of Bits

I pick bits of quotes and quips
of homemade savoury biscuits
of sketch books and sewing kits
of awkwardly shy party tricks
of the things I forget to do lists
of calamities and hissy fits
of impeccably perfect manners tips

of loose weaves and tight knits
of those I've known and dearly miss
of virtually ancient chart hits
of leaden skies and stormy bliss
of bits of that and bits of this
of bits and bobs and bits of bits!

A Note to the Editors

Those who dare to take a life out
of context, only to cut and paste
in a box... are sure to appreciate
not, that every person will take to
their end a full, uncensored plot.

Her Fuchsias of Fuchsia

Her nature was fuchsia with

her pale lips of

fervour, that soothed her and

moved her, in

view of her future, living finely

yet fuller with

fusions of fuchsias, that often

were nurtured

as if - they grew through her.

Crystal

Crystal had forgiven her youth
for the tangents of her mind.

For the many errors of judge-
ment that she had left behind.

For believing that she must be
the one who was always right.

Numerous fortunes had helped
her to reflect all shades of light.

A Button for Bliss

If chaos was appearing to take its toll
he'd duly press 'Control'.
To fend off all his problems in haste
he'd press 'Backspace'.
In attempt to change a miserable fate,
he'd soon press 'Escape'.
In order to give his spirits a decent lift
he'd often press 'Shift'.
Desperate to leave a sinking fleet, he'd
quickly press 'Delete'.
Those functions got him out of a mess,
but he'd rather find the
button for 'Uninterrupted Happiness'!

These Doubts

I can't walk through walls
and drift with the clouds or
sink into the sand but I can
work through my doubts.

I can't lose what's not been
found or scream without a
sound, but I doubt that my
doubts won't be worked out.

I shan't tap dance upside
down, around a strange town,
with undoubtful handfuls
of doubtless new doubts.

Hidden in Her Conscience

Hidden in her conscience is a
silent songstress, grasping on
for a 'fullness of wholeness',
as a penniless witness of the
'sweetness of richness', softly
sewn by a nimble seamstress
who refuses to be careless
while tranquil in her quietness,
in the hush of her calmness
both resisting and refusing
to be listless, to be feckless

Something Years Young!

You'll never be quite as old as you've
been told, because you're merely as
young as you've become, and you're
only as old as life unfolds, which is
only as old as young! You being one,
who's whatever years young, Bravo!
Before you know it, it'll be over and
done, with a happy return or a tonne.

My Favourite Discontinued Scent

Only
as
I
settle
for
the
least
that
is
left
of
what
is
not
to
last,
do
I
savour
the
most
of
what
is
meant
of
what
has
passed.

Tea

When quite enough is quite
enough and beyond enough
to be, a cup of self-worth, a
cup of rebirth, and the most
of the best and least of the
worst, I'm inclined to brew a   tea.

Words

Worn words hang knowingly in your closet.
Heavy words strain the lining of your pockets.
New words require a substantial deposit.

Dominant words deal and delve and dare.
Abrupt words halt the unassuming atmosphere.
Embarrassed words implode upon a stare.
Painful words ache beyond compare.

Blissful words lie lazily beneath your pillow.
Blinding words suit the poorly sighted armadillo.
Tormented words wisp between the leaves
of the weeping willow.

Rigid words never have any gear.
Chatty words evolve in the classroom rear.
Wild words roar and hiss and sneer.

Creepy words lurk eerily behind the nooks.
Lost and stolen words may find themselves in books.
Abusive words discredit themselves like crooks.

Exaggerated words make a situation worse.
Contemplative words ponder each chapter, line
and verse.
Shy words wish longingly to converse.

Rebellious words strive fiercely to disengage.
Tentative words are difficult to gauge.
Furious words seep through the page – with
undiluted rage.

Sharp words cut to the bone.
Tender words prefer a gentle tone.
Ambivalent words converge, diverge then moan.

Stroppy words should be left a blinkin'-lone!

Love Can Be

          the faintest
instance, from the furthest
distance, that appears in a
lost destiny, and the divine
wisdom that has long been
hidden beneath the weight
of calamity

Author's Notes

I would never have believed that writing poems would open up *so many* opportunities for me. For a start, it is through publishing and reviewing poetry online, that I have made fabulous and interesting friends from different walks of life, across the world. Over the years, I've been fortunate enough to have my poetry aired on two London radio stations where I have also been interviewed about my work. An initiative that began during the first Covid lockdown period was my collaborations with a number of very talented musicians, some of whom I've never actually met in person!

Furthermore, I have had the pleasure of participating in various Spoken Word events across London which inspired me to produce a series of three poetry shows with a collective of poets and musicians at the Tara Theatre in South London. One winter, a local community radio presenter actually paid me to recite my poetry at a social event.

As a poet who rarely enters competitions, I was over the moon when one of my poems won 900 pounds in a national poetry competition for a local mental wellbeing, community support group. This leads me to mention how gratifying it was to get a poem published in an anthology comprising of short stories, poems and artwork by contributors from the London borough where I live. It has also been a great honour to have recited my work at the Playfest of the Wimbledon International Music Festival.

I therefore hope that those like myself, who have never considered themselves to be especially talented or creative, will nonetheless keep "having a go" as well, and follow their pursuits in spite of the challenges they may face.

About the Author

Sheema Huq is a poet and lyricist who resides in London, England. She first entered the world of work almost 40 years ago and has undertaken roles such as project leader for a disability youth recreation service and charity retail manager. Over the years, she has enjoyed travelling in the UK and across the world. Presently she is a carer for her mother which she considers to be one of the greatest honours of her life.

Printed in Great Britain
by Amazon

61699201R00051